I0639597

Anna Olcott Commelin

Of such is the kingdom and other poems

Anna Olcott Commelin

Of such is the kingdom and other poems

ISBN/EAN: 9783337135621

Printed in Europe, USA, Canada, Australia, Japan

Cover: Foto ©Andreas Hilbeck / pixelio.de

More available books at **www.hansebooks.com**

OF SUCH IS THE KINGDOM,

AND OTHER POEMS.

BY

ANNA OLCOTT COMMELIN.

" Heaven lies about us
·in our infancy."

NEW YORK:
FOWLER & WELLS CO.,
27 EAST 21st STREET.
1894.

DEDICATION.

TO MY SONS.

Still through life's dim, uncertain maze I go,
In care and toil and burden of the day,
Yet in the mists and clouds of dun and gray,
Which compass as I wander to and fro,
Like golden halo of an after-glow,
Flooding with radiance a darkened way,
Cleaving the shadows with transcendent ray,
Thou, hallowed light of memory, doth show.
Thy home to-day may be in starry space,
Thou, who, on earth, brought message from above,
And thou, so loyal, gentle, brave and true,
O spirits rare from that high, heavenly place,
Still come with the old beauty and old love
To her who listens, longs and seeks for you.

TABLE OF CONTENTS.

7

OF SUCH IS THE KINGDOM.

" Heaven lies about us in our infancy."

OF SUCH IS THE KINGDOM.

O, all the little children,
  That this green earth have trod,
A blessing on their presence !
  They are so near to God !
We are so far from Heaven,
  They are so near to God.

The guileless little children,
  So innocent and wise,
Another world than ours,
  Around about them lies.
The happy little children,
  That frolic o'er the sod,
They are so near to Heaven,
  We are so far from God.

O, trust of little children !
  O faith to them made known !
This earth without their presence,
  Would be but drear and lone.

11

The happy little children !
   They come like flowers in May,
The winsome little children,
   Who gambol all the day.
Then when the light is fading,
   Their weary heads they nod ;
They are so near to Heaven,
   We are so far from God.

But oh for sorrow's children,
   Who throng the crowded street !
From attic and from cellar,
   They come with naked feet.
Oh, haggard men and women,
   And ye who ceaseless plod,
Take heed for these your children,
   They came to you from God.
They may be far from Heaven,
   They came to you from God.

The fragile little children,
   By holy angels sent,
They come with benediction,
   For briefest season lent.
They cannot linger with us,
   We cannot hold them long,
They see the courts of Heaven,
   And hear celestial song ;
The light of God's own glory,
   Is in their shining eyes.

They bring with them the halo,
 From stars of Paradise.
But blest the home forever,
 Where these shall enter in ;
That home is sacred, holy,
 Where such as these have been.
Oh, wounded hearts and breaking,
 That ache beneath the rod,
We nearer grow to Heaven,
 When these have gone to God !

MISCELLANEOUS POEMS.

"Thought is deeper than all speech,
Feeling deeper than all thought."

NIAGARA.

Niagara! Niagara! the wonder of the West!

The gleaming falls, the cliffs and stream, the rapids'
    wild unrest,

The glory of the cataract, the leaping torrent's play,

O'er chrysolyte and beryl hues ascends the snowy
    spray.

O majesty and marvel of the waters, who shall tell,

But one who dwells beside them and who lives within
    their spell.

The river, ceaseless flowing on, binds inland sea to sea,

From Erie's heights descending swift, its current
    dashes free.

O'er rocks and shales the rapids rush and curl in foam
    and crest—

Niagara! Niagara! the wonder of the West!

Niagara! Niagara! the monarch of the West!

On! on! the jeweled waves obey their ruler's stern
    behest.

And moving, foaming, dashing by, a crystal tide, they
    throng,

Till, in the brimming torrent's midst, they blend and
    glide along.

A sheen and maze of opaline, of sparkle and of glance,

And motion's magic mystery, in waves that sway and dance.

But soon the giant Horseshoe, in his robes of chrysoprase,

The sapphire waves, the iris crests in beauty doth surpass.

From far and near thy regal sway earth's pilgrims have confessed,

Niagara! Niagara! the monarch of the West!

Niagara! Niagara! the pride of all the West!

The mountains and the meadows, in their summer beauty drest,

No fairer hues display than show within the torrent's sheen

Where cymophane and amber glow in waters hyaline.

And regal in magnificence, adown the precipice,

The ermined monarch flings his wealth into the dread abyss.

And yet near Erie's fount in peace the gentle ripples glide,

Where green the islands fleck their glass, and currents slow divide.

But narrow grows the stream, and swift the foaming rapids break,

As onward, ever onward still, their ceaseless course they take,

To join the snowy cataract, the dizzy maelstrom's whirl,

And down, far down the rocky heights, the sparkling
    opals hurl.
While over all a fairy mist ascends and rises high,
And heaven seals earth's grandeur with a rainbow in
    the sky.
And all who see thy majesty, thy beauty still attest,
Niagara! Niagara! the pride of all the West!

Niagara! Niagara! the wonder of the West!
What tragedies, what mysteries are hid within thy
    breast!
An older myth still lingers of the maiden of the mist.
The red men with Niagara had held a sacred tryst,
For, year by year, in council here, they held their
    sacrifice;
Of all the tribes was chosen one, most beauteous in
    their eyes,
And once the chieftain's daughter was the fairest of
    the fair;
They placed her in a white canoe, and loosed her flow-
    ing hair.
Then, crowning her with blossoms sweet, they sped
    her on her way,
To brave the circling whirlpool and to die amid its
    spray.
The chieftain made no murmur as the fatal hour drew
    near,
No grief was on his features grave, his eyes betrayed
    no fear.

The white canoe, the white canoe, drawn onward by
    the tide,
Had neared the foaming rapids where Death waited
    for his bride,
But swift the chieftain followed on, and when the
    maid went o'er
The cataract, in his light bark, he plunged to rise no
    more.
And since that day, a spirit maid oft at the torrent's
    base,
Disporting in the spray and mist, displays her pallid
    face.
And there the naiad waits the forms of those who
    come to dwell
Beneath Niagara's seething foam, the victims of its
    spell.
What tragedies, what mysteries are hid within thy
    breast,
Niagara! Niagara! the wonder of the West!
Niagara! Niagara! from every land and clime,
Thy lovers come to learn in thee of Nature's ways
    sublime.

A NATIONAL FLOWER.

Glory of woodland and torrent,
  Glory of mountain and sea,
Glory of meadow and prairie,
  Land of the loyal and free,
Columbia, youthful and regal,
  With pride looketh forth over thee.

Northward and East, to the Southward,
  Out to the far spreading West,
Stretches her peerless dominion,
  Her glory by nations confessed,
Columbia, youthful and regal,
  Columbia, blessing and blest.

Blossoms perennial round her,
  Carpet with velvet her way,
Nature, her lavish hand-maiden,
  Crowns her as queen of the May ;
Columbia, youngest and fairest,
  She crowneth with garlands each day.

21

What brightest bloom shall we bring her,
  Jewel that time shall not tine?
Culled from her wealth of gay blossoms,
  One flower, the chosen and fine,
For Columbia, youngest and fairest,
  One flower as symbol and sign.

Wealth of America's flowers,
  In endless procession,—make room,
Room for the lilies, the roses,
  And violets breathing perfume,
For Columbia, regal in beauty,
  For bloom that shall rival her bloom.

Daisies and clematis, laurel,
  Buttercups sparkling in dew,
Sweet mignonette and white jasmine,
  Heartsease and arbutus too.
Bring, for Columbia's choosing,
  Wonders of beauty and hue.

Daffodils, lilacs, carnations,
  Wind-flower, lifting its head
Up, while the bleak winds are sighing,
  Out from its cold winter bed,
Strew, with her own floral tributes,
  The path where Columbia shall tread.

Flowers from far Colorado,
    Orchids with butterfly's wing,
Iris and primrose and aster ;
    Garlands from Florida bring,
For Columbia garlands and blossoms,
    Tell of perpetual spring.

Fruit trees in splendor before her,
    Deck themselves in the spring-tide,
Masses of glory of blossom,
    As if to adorn her as bride,
Columbia, youngest and fairest,
    Columbia, our queen and our pride.

France hath her fleur-de-lis stately,
    England her emblem,—the rose,
Scotland her brave, hardy thistle,
    What bloom for Columbia glows ?
For Columbia, queen of the nations,
    What flower for Columbia blows ?

Lily, with purest white chalice,
    Rare cup with its fragrance so faint,
What art and what pencil the finest,
    Thy beauty celestial can paint?
In Columbia's garden of flowers,
    We hold thee as bloom for a saint.

Roses, O wealth of the roses,
  That blush in their leafy green shade,
Finer their robing than raiment,
  Of velvet or satin sheen made.
For Columbia's matrons bring roses,
  In the pride of their beauty arrayed.

Wafting its incense around it,
  In jewel of emerald set,
Fragile and modest blue flower,
  With dew in the long grasses wet,
For Columbia's youth and fair maidens,
  We choose thee, thou sweet violet.

Bloom, O bright bloom universal,
  Spring-time and summer and fall,
Bloom on the cliff or the prairie,
  Bloom by the wayside stone wall,
For Columbia's richest and poorest,
  A flower that bloometh for all.

Low in the marsh doth it flourish,
  Up on the Alpine heights cold,
Scaling their battlements rocky,
  Planting its bannerets bold,
For Columbia's peerless dominion,
  It waveth its corymbs of gold.

Bloom, fitting type for a nation,
  Regal and strong,—'neath the sun,
Sturdy and brave as its people,
  Emblem more fitting is none,
Thou, like Columbia's subjects,
  Diverse and changing, art one.

Wand of a fairy thy courage,
  Wresting its wealth from the sod,
Turning the earth into treasure
  Of gold where thy feathered plumes nod,
For Columbia, strong and yet regal,
  Fit emblem art thou, golden-rod.

Thou art no bloom evanescent,
  Ethereal charm of a day,
Brave in the blast of November,
  As blithe in the sunshine of May,*
Emblem of strength that endureth,
  Type of Columbia's sway.

Flower for the poor and the lowly,
  Flower for the stateliest dame,
Ancient as legend of Druids,
  Symbol of union thy name,†
Thy thousand stars, golden and regal,
  Shall tell of Columbia's fame.

* The golden-rod blooms in different parts of the United States
from May until November.

† The botanical name of this flower is *Solidago*, from the verb
solidari, to unite.

25

Emblem and sign and true symbol,
    Free as Columbia's air,
Beautiful, hardy and stately,
    Finer than flowers more rare,
For Columbia thou art the emblem,
    Columbia, regal and fair.

A TREASURE.

It may be in a palace grand,
  It may be in a cot,
The hut is richer where it dwells,
  Than courts where it is not.

More to be prized than Ceylon's pearl,
  Than ruby or than gem,
Than sapphire blue or stones that deck
  A monarch's diadem.

The gold of Ophir scattered wide
  This gift can never bring,
Nor countless silver coins that make
  A ransom for a king.

We see it here, we find it there,
  We know it by a sign,
More precious than the jacinth's flame,
  From Oriental mine.

Sometimes a word will tell us where,
  This treasure hath its place,
And oft it shines in mothers' eyes,
  Or lights a child's fair face.

Who once hath known it counts its worth,
  All earthly goods above,
In castled halls, by lowly hearths,
  This priceless thing is love.

SUMMER FRIENDS.

In the dusk twilight of the summer day,
   Ere nature sank in deep repose of night,
While lingered touches of the sun's warm ray,
   For the first time they burst upon my sight.

In emerald robing, sweeping o'er the ground,
   Noble, majestic, rising grand and tall,
With gravest aspect, and in silence bowed,
   Stood one, unmoved, a king among them all.

And one, resplendent in her loveliness,
   Waved friendly greeting as I passed her by,
Woven of green and copper was her dress,
   Blent with the hue of roses in the sky.

Shy little faces hiding from my sight,
   In velvet hoods of purple and of gold,
Yet peering forth with bashful glances bright,
   Your looks a sweet and tender welcome told.

And through the grass another hither came,
   With furtive step, a timid, welcome guest,
Oft had I heard his dear familiar name,
   Oft had I seen his brilliant crimson vest.

28

O vision peerless, from what starry sphere,
  To earth in matchless splendor didst thou stray ?
Like angel visitant in slumber near,
  Who vanisheth at dawning of the day.

Friends were ye all, O spruce and copper beech,
  Pansies and bird and wondrous white-robed flower,*
Who came like messenger divine to teach
  Celestial ministry at midnight hour.

———

*Night-blooming Cereus.

AN UPLIFT.

At the turn of the road, on the hill's airy crest,
  In the upland so fair, is a cool spot I know,
Where, the steep climbing done, oft I tarry to rest,
  And to gaze, looking down, on the valley below.

For the heights are all scaled, and the vision is won,
  And above brightly gleams the expanse of deep
    blue,
While the peaks of the mountains are gold in the sun,
And the lush grass is fresh with the morning's pure
  dew.

And I stand, and I linger beside a stone wall,
  Where the flowers are peeping through each crevice
    low,
Where the poppies, sweet-pease, and the hollyhocks
  tall
And the violets, pinks and the red roses blow.

Then I breathe in, I live in this wealth of bright bloom,
  And I fill with a marvel of color my eyes,
While the breezes are wafting their incensed perfume,
  On the hill's verdant crest, where the old garden
    lies.

Then how short seems the way to the plain once
  again,
And the mists of the valley no longer I see,
In the mart, with the throng and the tumult of men,
  All the view of the upland I carry with me.

A WOMAN'S NAME.

Sometimes, amid the whirl of life,
   There comes a thought to me,
Have I as child, as maid or wife,
   A personality ?

And oft the question will arise
   To puzzle and to vex,
Nor comfort find I 'neath the skies,
   In order nor in "Lex."

A happy child, no name I knew
   But "Kit" or "Puss," although
The register baptismal, true,
   Rose Katharine Poor, would show.

Then on my tombstone, should I die,
   In words both sad and dour,
It would be writ, "Here rests for aye
   The offspring of John Poor."

But when I grew in maiden grace,
   And learned to bake and stitch,
In matrimony's honored place
   I changed to Mrs. Rich.

But from my side my mate was torn,
　　Alas! in one short year,
And left me, widowed and forlorn,
　　To weep upon his bier.

And if my time to die had come,
　　Inscribed in lesser niche,
It had been writ upon his tomb,
　　The "relict of John Rich."

But blooming youth revives again,
　　And when some time had fled,
I heard soft pleadings, not in vain,
　　Another love to wed.

And now again, as Mrs. Brown,
　　I'm puzzled as of old,
Whene'er I hear, around the town,
　　My names in order told.
And is it I, or is it not?
　　Chameleon-like is woman's lot!

THE POET'S GIFT.

The vision lieth in his brain,
The marvel seen on mount or plain,
  On rugged height or flowered lea,
The seasons' wonders, as they roll,
With subtle meaning fill his soul.
  The tender lights on land or sea
With pictured shapes and forms appear,
And music floats upon his ear,
But in his thought it lingers long,
Before it bursts in joy to song,
  And cadences of melody.

Vibrant to beauty everywhere,
Like harp Eolian to the air,
  The poet hears each repetend,
But quick to feel and quick to know,
Each wailing note of human woe.

As flashing sword from scabbard leaps,
At tale for which a soldier weeps,
So, with injustice, human ills,
The seer's heart responsive thrills ;
His bugle note for freedom rings,
And clarion the lay he sings,
  A man and brother to defend.

The poet broods on mystery
Of life that is, and life to be,
   On quiet he doth often wait,
While science seeks the ways of God,
Wresting from rock and wave and sod,
And here and there she finds a gem,
And binds it in a diadem
   To lighten the sad brow of fate.

But, inward borne, the avatar
May see a glory from afar ;
Like prophet in the days of old,
To him a splendor is foretold,
   His eyes have entered Heaven's gate.

THE LIGHT WITHIN.

Traveler, as thou passest by
Where the roads diverging lie,
Which one choosest thou, and why?

Right or left or straight ahead,
Which the path thy steps shall tread?
By what motive art thou led?

As I look upon thy face,
In its features can I trace
Aught of comfort to thy race?

Findest thou in church and creed
All the help that thou dost need,
Guidance sure thy steps to lead?

Creeds by mortals were designed.
In them thou shalt never find
Trace of an Almighty mind.

Dost thou find in human love
Joy all other joys above,
Stay where'er thy steps may rove?

35

Human love its course may run,
Death may take thy dearest one,
Turning into night thy sun.

Seek within thyself thy stay !
True unto thy soul, thy way
Shall be lit with some bright ray.

But thou sayest, Age will chill ;
Slowly on, with footsteps still,
Comes the messenger of ill.

Then, where findest thou the light,
When the soul's enclouded sight
Falters in the coming night?

Then, the banquet o'er, thy place
Thou must learn to leave with grace :
Thou hast had this life's brief space.

But, when tenement of clay
Fails and falters day by day,
Yet shows fair the spirit's sway,—

Softly falling evening's shade,
Yet thy soul in light arrayed,
In thyself shalt thou be stayed !

LIFE.

In a mist of of tulle and laces, garlanded with flowers
　　rare,
With a crown of orange blossoms twined above her
　　golden hair,
And a face of sculptured beauty, she is fairest of the
　　fair.

And her blue eyes, shy and tender,, all their depth of
　　feeling show,
When her lover's words, soft-spoken, fall like music,
　　sweet and low,
And her cheeks, before like lilies, now with blushing
　　roses grow.

"Life," she thought, "hath girlhood dreaming e'er
　　foretold such joy as thine ?
Fondest fancies, brightest visions, in fulfillment all are
　　mine,
And the glowing future opens, with its promises di-
　　vine."

From the gay and festal portal passed the youthful,
    happy bride.
With the sacred ring espousal, and her husband by her
    side,
Out from love, parental, shielding, to the new love
    glorified.

But within the nearest mansion, where the bridal
    comers' tread
Echoed to the sound of music, robed in black, with
    drooping head,
Sat a woman, wan and hopeless, from whom love and
    joy had fled.

" Life," she said, " the saddest fancy, saddest fears by
    boding wrought,
Doubts and black Despair's betrayals, offspring born
    of darkest thought,
All, to what thou bringest, phantom, cruel phantom,
    Life, are nought."

But when came the midnight stillness, in its hush a
    presence dear,
Messenger of balm and healing, seemed to hover, bend-
    ing near,
Clothed in fairest spirit beauty ; thus it spake, in
    accents clear :

"Knowest thou that, often, Sorrow, when away she
    takes from thee
Joy and gladness, yet permitteth light divine thine eyes
    to see?
I am near thee, ever near thee, thou canst draw more
    near to me.

"But a veil of mist divides us; couldst thy vision
    clearer show,
Forms of spirit life revealing, all thy tears would cease
    to flow,
And the life that I have entered, The Eternal thou
    shalt know."

ONE SOUL.

A slender woman toiled with care each day,
To cheer and help the needy on their way,
Children she taught and tried their hearts to win,
And women save from ignorance and sin.

With lofty aim and consecrated will,
She strove, in love, to lessen human ill,
And, as she toiled, the field still wider grew,
The more she strove, the more she saw to do.

One summer day she trod the heated street,
Weary and worn she sped, with aching feet.
A friend she met; "What hast thou done?" said he,
"What human soul hast saved from misery?

"Thou givest thought unto a thankless band,
And yet thou canst not show in all the land
One life made happy." This the cynic said:
"Then take thine ease." She raised her drooping
    head,

And spoke: "My heart responds to others' needs,
Though weak may be my aid to their good deeds,
But I am glad, if for this cause alone,
From sordid life one soul I've saved—my own."

MY VALENTINE.

Maid : Miss Lucy, I have caught you !
  You've got a valentine !
That college student sent it,
  Who comes sometimes to dine.

I've seen his black eyes sparkle !
  I think him very bold,
And you in your short dresses—
  Your mother shall be told.

Lucy: You're getting quite too saucy,
  And putting on such airs !
Go back into the nursery,
  And mind your own affairs.

Lucy (reads) : " Your eyes are blue as sapphires,
  As black as sloes are mine :
Your cheeks are like twin roses,
  O, be my valentine !"

Lucy (aloud) : Give me black eyes forever,
  I choose them every time.
Maid (aside) : It is the black-eyed student;
  He writes to her in rhyme !

Oh, I shall tell her mother !
　　I'm sure she doesn't know !
Miss Lucy in short dresses—
　　And still she has a beau !

　　　　　　　　[*Exit maid.*

Lucy : She's gone at last !　I'm thankful !
　　She says she'll tell mamma !
And then she thinks this evening,
　　Mamma will tell papa !
But I must write my letter,
　　Before she comes again,
If she comes back, how tiresome !
　　It all will be in vain.

Lucy writes :　" Your eyes are soft as velvet,
　　When they look into mine ;
Give me black eyes forever !
　　I am your valentine."

Lucy : Now, where are my envelopes ?
　　I'll look them through and through,
To find one worth the sending
　　To you, my sweetheart true.
Here's one will well disguise me,
　　I think that it will do.

Now I shall run to post it
　　Before mamma can view.
O, what a joke ! my valentine—

"Give me black eyes forever"—
    Is black-eyed Cousin Sue !
    For her my billet-doux.
We school-girls play at lovers :
    Dear Cousin Sue is mine,
    And I'm her valentine !

HISTORY AND HEART HISTORIES.

I leave the storied page of history,
    The vain ambition of a Bonaparte,
With tales of slaughter, battles lost or won,
    And all of warfare's gory, savage art.

But in some lonely, country by-way oft,
    As on an unfrequented road I stray,
I pause beside an humble little plot,
    With grassy mounds and hoary tombstones gray.

The daisies nod, and green the grasses wave,
    While through the field alone I softly tread,
And bending low above the ancient mounds,
    I read the sacred records of the dead.

Long years have flown, but oft a tribute fair,
    A rose in bloom, a flower or a wreath,
Tell me the story of a living love,
    For one whose form lies in the dust beneath.

Sorrow and love, life's anguish and its crown,
    With these to-day each mortal still hath part!
I leave the wars, the hates of history,
    And read, ofttimes, these stories of the heart!

44

THE GHOST OF PERIANDER'S WIFE.

The wife of Periander,
  When she crossed o'er the Styx,
Bore with her royal raiment
  Of garments rare and rich.
No ghost e'er owned such wardrobe,
  Nor woman, strange to say,
Not even Miss McFlimsey,
  Can boast such robes to-day.

This ruler, Periander,
  Lived centuries ago,
Before the Saviour's coming,
  As history doth show.
The friend of art and learning,
  But "tyrant" was his name;
He killed his wife, Melissa,
  And lived in evil fame.

No honor then he paid her,
  No funeral pyre had she,
Melissa, born a princess,
  And called the honey-bee.
Her body and her garments,
  Were buried in the glade,
No smoke of burning raiment,
  Ascended to her shade.

Ended was fair Melissa,
  So Periander deemed,
Of stinging bees returning,
  The tyrant never dreamed.
It happened that a stranger,
  To Corinth once had brought
A treasure rich : he hid it;
  And, lest it should be sought,

He told none but Melissa.
  To find this treasure rare,
The sordid Periander,
  Was seeking here and there.
With bribes and threats his workmen,
  Were sent the country round,
In byway and through highway,
  They harried all the ground.

But vain was all their searching,
  And Periander cried,
"The Gods above will help us,
  The oracles will guide."
So, speeding to Dodona,
  The messengers were sent,
To groves of Hesprotia,
  With anxious haste they went.

They poured, with rites, libations,
  And offered sacrifice,
And, trembling, waited rustling
  Of leaves, for their replies.

Out of the mists of evening,
   That shrouded all the place,
Framed in a wreath of oak leaves,
   There rose a wan, pale face.

With hollow voice, Melissa
   Unto the envoys said,
" Go, give to Periander
   A message from the dead."
They gazed in awe and doubting,—
   " His loaves in oven cold
Are put, and never, never,
   Shall any find that gold.

" Until he sends me clothing,
   For cold I wander here,
My garments all were buried,
   Not burned upon my bier.
He ne'er shall see that treasure,
   Nor know its hiding-place,
Until he makes atonement."
   Then vanished her pale face.

Plain message to the living,
   From ghost were words like these,
No need of tinkling symbols,
   Nor soughing winds in trees.
The envoys heard the message,
   They conned it o'er and o'er,
And speeding back to Corinth,
   Melissa's words they bore.

*   *   *   *   *   *

What stir there was in Corinth,
　　What flutter of delight,
In every Gynæceum,
　　Behold the chitons bright !
The open, scented wardrobes,
　　The silks, brocades and flowers,
The long-twined garlands fitting
　　For Flora's rosy bowers.

The prince had sent a crier
　　To tell the news to all,
That soon, in Hera's temple,
　　Should be a festival.
And every Corinth woman,
　　In robes of silk and lace,
Might crush a former rival,
　　And show her own fair face.

Then praise for Periander !
　　Bow down to princely sway,
All hail the ruler gracious
　　Who plans a festal day !
And then for poor Melissa,
　　They were so sorry too,
And meet it were and fitting,
　　To give her honor due.

It was a day of gladness,
　　The ether seemed to dance ;
Beneath their wreaths of roses,
　　How softly bright eyes glance !

Behold the lines of women,
　　From byway, street, and lane,
Maids, matrons, slaves, and peasants,
　　They press to Hera's fane!

The prince is seen approaching,
　　Announced by trumpets' blare.
" Long life to Periander ! "
　　Rings out upon the air.
" Long life to him, our ruler,
　　Who gives the holiday,
We wave for him our garlands,
　　We honor him," they say.

But he, the altar seeking,
　　Thus speaketh to them all :
" Ye who have loved Melissa,
　　Know what doth her befall.
A restless ghost she roameth,
　　Alone in nether air,
Too shy to follow Charon,
　　She wanders cold and bare.

" Now, every woman of you,
　　To expiate this wrong,
Give up the festal garments
　　That unto you belong.
So all the costly dresses,
　　Brocades and satin sheen,
In holocaust right fitting,
　　Shall burn for her, I ween.

"There's no escape! I leave you!
　　My guards are here! Beware!
　If one of you is niggard,
　　That one I shall not spare."
　O, then arose a wailing,
　　Resounding through the town,
"O, pity, Periander!
　　This is my wedding gown!"

"O, mercy, Periander!
　　This is my only dress!"
　They seized his robe; he cared not,
　　Nor heeded their distress.
　A wall of soldiers standing,
　　Before the temple wait.
"O, pity, Periander!"
　　They hear behind its gate.

　But Periander crieth,
"At once! or you I spurn!
　A gown for each! or with you
　　Your finery shall burn!"
　Then sounded stifled sobbing,
　　And from the portico,
　A silken tunic falleth,
　　And white arms trembling show.

　Then more white arms and shoulders
　　Brown, shapely ones are seen,
　And draggled flowers, sad faces,
　　With tear-stained ones between.

And heaped up high the tunics,
　The chitons of brocade,
With wealth of silk and color
　And rainbow sheen displayed.

The royal pile was lighted,
　Fit pyre for monarch's boast,
And humbly Periander,
　Invoked Melissa's ghost.
Then rose the clouds in volumes,
　As smoke from Etna's thrall,
And darkness covered Corinth,
　With sable shroud and pall.

Then none could see her neighbor,
　But in rich dress arrayed,
And dazzling in her splendor,
　Appeared Melissa's shade.
Peasants and slaves, maids, matrons,
　Disrobed, and faint with fright,
Melissa guided homeward,
　In cover of the night.

Again asked Periander,
　About the treasure-trove.
Melissa told the secret
　Unto her lord in love.
So avarice was sated,
　The strong oppressed the weak ;
A moral in this ending
　It would be vain to seek.

But all the Corinth merchants,
  Their stuff to women sold,
" Ill is the wind that blows no good,"
  Their coffers filled with gold.

L'ENVOI.

For man's injustice ever,
  Doth woman vainly weep ;
This tale refutes one slander :
  She may a secret keep !

POEMS IN SORROW.

" Something unfading, plucked from fading years,
Something to blossom on beyond the sun,
From Sorrow won."

AS ROUND THE EVENING LAMP WE SIT.

As round the evening lamp we sit,
The sombre twilight phantoms flit;
Away the wraiths of sadness glide,
Their haunting presence leaves my side,
And mocking shadows fade and flee.
The dusky shapes are all alight,
The room with softest glow is bright,
The labors of the day are o'er,
And, list! they enter at the door.
A fair, fair form is near to me,
O, then life's shades and sorrows flit,
As round the evening lamp we sit.

As round the evening lamp we sit,
Then heart and heart in ties are knit,
And tenderness shines soft in eyes,
And thought that deep, unspoken, lies,
Of day's hard battles, lost or won,
Comes forth awaiting love's replies,
As blossoms open to the sun,
And, in the telling, loss is less,
And, in the sharing, joys increase,
And crown the close of day with peace.
O, none on all the earth have power,
To mar the solace of the hour
Whose influence doth come to bless.
For heart and heart in ties are knit,
As round the evening lamp we sit.

As round the evening lamp we sit,
We chat with cheer and mirth and wit,
And one is in her crown of years,
And eager with youth's hopes and fears.
And beautiful a youthful pair,
Are side by side, and one—how fair!
The light shines on his curling hair.
An infant sweet is on my knee,
His velvet eyes are soft and deep,
Whether for life to smile or weep,
He knoweth not; to us who wait,
He cometh as a prince in state
The wonders of this world to see.
We chat, with cheer and mirth and wit,
As round the evening lamp we sit.

As round the evening lamp we sit,
The thronging faces come and flit.
The fire-light wanes, the lamp burns low,
Where are the eyes with love aglow?
Where are they, brown, and soft, and blue,
Where are the hearts that once beat true?
The young—the old—they all are gone!
A moment since, and they were here,
Where are they now—the dead and dear?
How dark it grows; the night is chill,
The empty room seems drear and still.
The flame is quenched; once more alone,
While shapes and shadows come and flit,
Beside the evening lamp I sit.

FOE OR FRIEND.

When I was but a child, so near he came,
    I felt his breath ;
I fled in fear, and trembled at his name,
    This monster, Death.

So sudden was his coming that I knew,
    No danger nigh,
Until my playmate at my side he slew.
    With bitter cry,

I saw my brother stretched upon his bier.
    I touched his face :
'Twas icy cold, I spake : he did not hear,
    Then, for a space,

I knew no more. They carried me away,
    The house was still.
How hushed it was, and strange it seemed each day
    With presence ill.

How deep the terror brooding over all !
    How dread the fear,
Lest once again the smiting bolt should fall,
    With Death so near !

I knew not that the awful phantom's face,
So stern, so grim,
Familiar grown, might show transfigured grace,
Some sign from Him.

Might show the marble majesty of peace,
When spent the breath;
The calm thou bringest to sharp pain's surcease,
O white-winged Death !

And if thy fearful touch and cold embrace,
My soul shall send,
To meet again my loved ones face to face,
Thou art my friend.

ONE ROOM.

IN MEMORIAM.

O silent room,
Where still the sunlight splendor falls
On rug and books and pictured walls.
The sunlight falls, the sunlight fades,
The bright day dawns, the evening shades,
But oh, thou silent, empty, room,
In sunlight bathed, thou'rt steeped in gloom!

O lonely room,
I listen, listen at its door,
But the light footfall sounds no more.
The sunlight falls, the sunlight fades,
The bright day dawns, the evening shades,
But morn and noon and eve are vain
To bring him to my arms again.

O saddest room!
All beautiful and cold and dead,
With lids down-dropped and spirit fled,
I see him here. O failing breath!
O pain and anguish, might of Death!

59

The sunlight falls, the sunlight fades,
The bright day dawns, the evening shades,
But glory of the fairest day
Can take nor pain nor grief away.

    O full, full room,
Hast thou, in all thy breadth, one space
Where see I not a fair young face?
Hast thou, in all thy length, one spot
Where, when I gaze, I see him not?
And list'ning, list'ning, accents sweet
I hear, with sound of eager feet.
The sunlight falls, the sunlight fades,
The bright day dawns, the evening fades,
In deepest gloom, in darkest night,
O sacred room, thou'rt bathed in light!

    O sacred room,
A room to love all consecrate,
Like shrine of old wherein I wait.
A fair, fair form before me lies,
A light of heaven in his eyes.
The sunlight falls, the sunlight fades,
The bright day dawns, the evening shades,
But of love, life, divinity,
O sacred room, thou'rt full to me.

IT LIETH LOW.

There's a grave upon the hillside,
  Low it lieth, lieth low ;
In the golden summer sunshine,
  When the autumn wind doth blow,
In the springtide bloom and promise,
  In the winter's falling snow,
There it lieth, lieth low.
  Ah, my heart it acheth so,
When I stand beside its grasses,
  By the grave that lieth low.

Yet whene'er away I wander
  From that grave that lieth low,—
When in fairest lands I loiter,
  Where the roses deepest glow,
And the flowers bloom eternal,
  And the skies their bluest show,—
Yet my heart it acheth so
  For the grave that lieth low.
Vain unrest to stray or wander
  From that grave that lieth low.

E'en though dear ones cluster round me,
   When afar away I go,
Comes the longing, oh, the longing,
   For the grave that lieth low,
Comes the fear lest death might smite me,
   Brimming o'er the cup of woe,
   Lest I may not lie below
Tangled ivies, myrtles, grasses,
   By the grave that lieth low.
   Ah, my heart it acheth so !

Close beside it, close beside it,
   By that grave that lieth low,
Let me lie at length in slumber,
   Slumber that we all shall know.
Where he lies, the brave and tender,
   Autumn wind the leaves doth strow,
   On that grave that lieth low.
   Ah, my heart it acheth so !

But if ever blessed spirit,
   Life of light and joy may sow,
Then he knows that joy forever,
   He whose form lies cold below,
With the saints in God's high heaven,
   Radiant in love's o'erflow.
Oh, my heart will fill with rapture,
   Once again his love to know.
   My poor heart that acheth so,
   From that grave that lieth low !

HOW SHALL IT BE?

How shall it be,
When life's warm tide is failing,
When the heart's throbbings faint and fainter grow,
And mortal weakness lays the body low,
When ebbs the breath,
And the stern angel, Death,
The hue of cheek is paling,
How shall it be,
How shall it be to me?

How shall it be?
Shall the brain cease its thinking?
Shall the eye close to sight it holds most dear?
Love's cadences fall silent on the ear,
Her sweetest word
No more, no longer heard,
All in oblivion sinking?
Thus shall it be,
Shall it be thus to me?

Or shall it be
A glorious awaking,
When the pure spirit bursts from bond of earth,
To life celestial, to the soul's new birth;
From deeps of night
To starry worlds of light,
Like dawn of day new breaking?
Thus may it be,
So may it be to me!

Oh may it be
The opening of the portal,
The dazzling, pearly gates of Paradise,
Supernal vision of the suns and skies.
Transcendent dawn,
The radiance of the morn
Of life, of life immortal,
Thus may it be,
Oh, may it be to me!

Oh, may it be
That, from those fairest places,
One shining one from heaven down may stray
To meet me, bear me on the upward way,
And, at the door,
The loved and lost once more
Shall smile with angel faces.
Thus may it be,
So may it be to me!

64

So may it be,

O, world of light, where never
Ah, nevermore hearts bow with sorrow's might,
But love shall know that love is infinite.

All things above,

Light, life and heaven and love,

The joy of love forever.

So may it be,

So may it be to me !

TWO DAYS.

So chill and damp, with heavy clouds of gray,
And mist and fog encircling earth to-day,
And Sorrow stalks abroad with Woe and Pain,
And hopes that promised fair have proved but vain;
And strength is turned to weakness, and our trust
Has wavered in the ones we deemed were just.
And friends, who take each other by the hand,
Will go their way, and still misunderstand.
O loved ones, whereso'er your dwelling be,
From that fair home, O come not back to me ;
To all the pain of this world's weary rack,
We would not, dearest, would not call ye back !

How glad the sunbeams shine again to-day—
The happy children frolic in their play,
The skies are blue, the gentle zephyrs blow,
The flowers bloom, and spring's sweet roses glow,
And youthful hearts with happiness beat high,
And bright-hued birds with joyous note flit by,
And music charms, and winged hours are fleet,
And life, this life, thou art so sweet, so sweet !
And friends are true, and hope, that once had fled,
Returns again.   O dearest ones, who tread,
To us, afar, an unknown, shining track,
Would, O belovèd, we could call ye back ?

We would not! O, we would! and which were best?
Had love the choosing at its own behest,
When life in losing these its all doth lack,
O would we, dare we, dearest, call ye back?

THE OPEN WAY.

Sometimes the way seems open, and my dear ones
  Are near to me as in the days of yore,
In sweet communing, in the same affection,
  My darlings come to visit me once more.

O eyes of blue, angelic in your sweetness,
  O glorious orbs of brown, so soft and true,
No more on earth they show to me in beauty
  The love, the trust, the tenderness I knew.

But oft I feel a blessed sense of presence,
  Around about me forms I cannot see ;
Upholding with their gentle ministration,
  As angel guides they walk and dwell with me.

Sometimes the veil seems almost to be parted,
  And wondrous powers unknown before unfold,
The fond pet names I hear once more repeated,
  Again we talk together as of old.

The very speech, familiar in its phrasing
  As household word, thrills on my listening ear,
And sacred prescience of spirit knowledge
  Which, in its ken, holds all our actions here.

O dead no more ! Ye are to us the living,
  Though past the bound of our dull mortal sight,
Enshrined in heart of love with the immortals,
  To dwell transfigured in their world of light !

A STAR IN THE NIGHT.

There came a Winter morn, when from the sky
The color faded, and the sun's bright ray
Seemed but to mock my soul's great agony.
Oh, desolate the room wherein each day
Had heart to heart responded, where love's speech
Had sounded in my ear, and sweet blue eyes,
All guileless in their trust, looked into mine.
Oh, desolate seemed all the things of earth
When that day broke.   The blackness of despair
Had settled into depth of changeless night.
Is there a God, I cried, when, in an hour,
Is shattered nature's fairest, finest work,
And ruthlessly asunder hearts are torn ?
No sound from out the stillness !   Silence all !
My ceaseless cry, my longing all in vain !
The light of life quenched in an endless night.
The slow weeks dragged their length, and month by
    month
The darkness thickened.   Through the murky gloom
A little ray, a faintest ray appeared.
As the poor prisoner, in the dungeon depth,
Doth catch one gleam of sunlight, so to me
There dawned reflection of a distant light.

Struggling and gazing upward then I sought
For clearer vision, seeking prop and staff
And crutch to aid me as I tried to climb.
When, lo ! a sign—a token—came to me—
A wondrous sign ! I stood, with bated breath,
My ear attuned to lightest sound revealed.
The star of Hope arose. Perchance, perchance,
A light at last doth penetrate the gloom.
He lives ! my own ! and near me, near me still,
He comes ! he comes ! to tell me of his love.
Oh, white-winged Hope divine ! sustaining Hope !
I follow thee, thou Heaven-sent angel guide !

Again the shaft doth fall ! the good, the fair,
The loved, the tender, true and beautiful,
With one fell blow are smitten, and they lie
Together in the cold embrace of death.
Not one, not one, my God, to bide with me !
Too gentle were they for a rough world's use,
But, oh ! the solitude for us who stay !
For whom the sunshine never beams so warm,
For whom the light of day and all things fair
Are darkened. But the guiding star of Hope
That led before doth beckon once again.
They are not lost, she says, nor gone so far
Into the heavenly way, they may not come
With message, and with token, and with sign,
That tell of love unchanging. Hark ! I hear
Those words of comfort. Still my heart
Doth find its echo in the hearts that love.

Oh, angels ministrant unto my need,
Who telegraph sweet words of sympathy,
No more am I alone, for, heart to heart,
We meet communing, and the door doth ope
That closed between the living and the dead.
From depths of darkness streams the living light.
A "cloud of witnesses" encompass us.
Behold, the universe hath changed its front,
And God himself doth manifest to man!

THEY SEEK US STILL.

We say "God-speed" to loved ones when they leave us
  For distant lands, beyond the ocean's wave,
But ever still for word and sign and token,
  That all is well our hearts expectant crave.

How do they fare, the well-beloved, the living,
  Who seek afar earth's wonders on their way?
We follow all their footsteps in their journey,
  And watch and wait their message day by day.

We lay our loved away, our dead and dearest—
  How fares the soul? our hearts in anguish cry.
"'Tis not for us to rend the veil of silence,"—
  Who ne'er have drank from sorrow's cup reply.

"Seek not communion with the world of spirits,
  And all thy unavailing efforts cease,
Turn thou to others, in the throng of living,
  Leave thou the dead to slumber and to peace."

The dead, who loved us, come again in longing!
  Would they be happy in some far-off sphere,
Estranged from all the tender ties once sacred,
  Which made of life its consecration here?

No! Still they love us! still they long to tell us,
  In wondrous ways, by message and by sign,
"All is not lost! we seek you as you seek us!"
  Wouldst thou shut out these messengers divine?

SHORT POEMS AND SONNETS.

" Awake thou, Lute and Harp."

MARCH.

Cold and drear, cold and drear,
Stormy March again is here.
His bleak winds are whistling by ;
Through the lonely woods they sigh ;
Wailing through each leafless tree,
Boreas, let loose, doth moan.
Ill the winds and ill alone,
Which no gifts to mortals bring.
Zephyrs tell of coming spring,
Wafting good to thee and me.
    Cold and drear, cold and drear,
    Boreas again is here.

SEPTEMBER.

September Days ! September Days !
    Wealth of the springtime and summer and fall,
Seedtime and blooming and harvest and all,
    Woodbine aflame on the old garden wall,
Scarlet and gold on each tree in a maze,
    Spring's fairest promise and midsummer haze,
Autumn's fruition, a pæan of praise !
    Ever her changes of wonder to ring,
Gladly an anthem to nature we sing.
    Life hath its autumn and summer and spring.
Richer and riper as on goeth time,
    Harvest of gold the meridian's prime,
Weave for the fullness of promise a rhyme !
    Woodland and roadside in beauty ablaze,
Golden-rod gleams in the sun's slanting rays,
    September days ! September days !

IN SUMMER TIME.

RONDEAU.

In summer time, in sunny lane,
Roamed Cupid, armed with barb of pain,
Seeking a maid, whose cheeks glowed red,
At sound of Cupid's lightest tread ;
With tender word he sought to gain,
Her glances sweet, in sunny lane,
The while he aimed his barb of pain,
     In summer time.

The flowers were fresh with softest rain,
The chestnut blooms were gold again,
The bee hummed o'er the clover bed,
The poppy drooped its drowsy head,
The light breeze swayed the ripened grain,
And Cupid thought that he would wed,
The sweet fair maid, in sunny lane,
     In summer time.

The warm, warm days were on the wane,
The chill blast broke the summer's reign,
The blossoms fell, the leaves were dead,
And where was Love? With wings outspread,
To pastures new had Cupid sped.
From the maid's cheek the bloom had fled,
And tears had left their passing stain,
But plaint and sigh and tears were vain,
To the sweet maid of sunny lane,
Past like a lute's forgotten strain,
  Was summer time.

FAR AND NEAR.

We sit beside the same hearth-stone,
We watch the fire-light's rosy glow,
And see the shadows come and go.
We hear, without, the wind's low moan,
And see the curtains drawn within.
The evening lamp's soft, steady light
Falls on the rug, with colors bright,
And hushed is all the city's din.
How close we sit ! Almost, I think,
I feel thy breath upon my face,
While, in the old, accustomed place,
The evening cup of cheer we drink.
Night after night, day after day,
So passes life's short span away.
So near to me, so near to me,
Thou knowest me not ; I know not thee.
My soul to thee has bolt and bar,
Thou art so near, and yet so far.
And one is tossed on stormy sea,
So far away, so far away.
Night after night, day after day,
I think of him, he thinks of me.
Wild wastes of waters us divide,

And cruel distances amain
Lengthen the weary way again,
With billow and untoward tide.
Fair light of home, the evening cheer,
The warm glow on the hearth-stone wide,
The cup of kindness, side by side,
Are lost by distances so drear,
Yet ever, ever with me here,
He, though so far, is yet so near.

PSYCHE.

Word fraught with meaning,—need we not to seek,
  As time its course shall ceaseless onward roll,
A fairer thought than thine—prophetic Greek—
  Which gave the butterfly the name of soul.
From lethargy of chrysalis and night,
Its airy wings ascend to life and light.

So when the failing body yields its breath,
  And scenes of earth have faded from the view,
Out from the lethargy and night of death
  May the pure spirit burst to glories new,
Leaving its faded chrysalis below,
Soaring, to mount, a fairer life to know.

To O. L. B.

IN THE DAYS GONE BY.

Blue the water's broad expanse,
　　Bluer still the sky,
Bright the flowers, fleet the hours
　　Of the days gone by.

Summer days and autumn days,
　　Wealth of bloom anigh,
Azure lakes and ferns and brakes,
　　In those days gone by.

Barberries the wayside flame,
　　Hills around so high,
Asters blow and fruit-trees glow,
　　In the days gone by.

Maid and youth in life's spring dream,
　　Sweet the friendship tie,
Golden dawn of fairest morn,
　　Ah, those days gone by !

———

May the days that are to come
　　Lack no good for thee,
May they bring fair blossoming,
　　Days that are to be.

THE POET AND THE WORLD.

The poet, fresh from glimpse of Helicon,
Carried that vision in his inmost soul,
With joy that overflowed itself to all.
As down the market-place he strolled one day,
He met the merchant counting o'er his gains,
And him accosted with such grace of speech,
The merchant thought he needs must ask an alms,
Else why did he expend his art in words?
He scanned the threadbare coat, and thought he
     begged,
And roughly spurned, and sent him on his way.
Chagrined, the poet turned: "He knows me not!
I ask an alms? 'Twas friendship that I craved,"
And solitary passed he on his way.

The poet chose a woman for a friend,
Aghast to find in man such sordid mind.
He talked to her of love,—of love divine
Which glorified the humble, lowly cot,
And made its grace transcend a palace gilt.
O love of man for man, in friendship true!
O love of mate for mate! for little child!
O love that bindeth heart to heart where'er
'Tis manifest, and love aglow o'er all,
The universal pulsing love divine.

The woman knew not of a love so large,
And sought, with tie, to bind him to her side.
" Deceiver art thou ! " thus, with bitter word,
The poet-soul she wounded, till at length
He shrank again to solitary ways.

The poet wrote of things to him revealed,
And scattered all the wealth to him made known.
" He but imagines," then the people said ;
Did he hear voices from the spirit world ?
With jeer and taunt they tried to bind him down
To form and creed and sacerdotal rite.
O poet, find a friend with poet-soul,
Else shall thy path be evermore alone !

LIFE ?

Art thou but essence from the earth that springs
In beauty to the rose's fragrant bloom,
That opes it dewy leaves and breathes perfume,
Then falls and perisheth : in bird that sings
With joyous note and plumes his rainbow wings
For one brief day, then fadeth into gloom ;
In man, who climbs to heights, then reads the doom
That nature to her fair creation brings ?
Or art thou immanent in lowly clod,
Art thou in chrism of bud and blossom fine,
Power that worketh wonders from the sod,
The innermost revealed in eyes that shine ?
Is life, our life, but part of life of God,
Which we shall find again in life divine ?

FEET OF CLAY.

She thought her idol was of gold—pure gold,
From noble forehead down to shapely feet,
Wrought of rich ore, and clothed in raiment meet
That draped his kingly form with sweeping fold.
His curling locks from his broad brow were rolled,
The lips were parted in smile's semblance sweet,
When low she bent his favor to entreat,
And never blemish marred the perfect mould.
His robe of minever was clasped with gem,
An aureola glowed about his head;
Prostrate she knelt, until, by chance, one day,
She turned aside the flowing garment's hem,
Lest all too near her timid steps should tread :—
Behold, her idol's feet were made of clay !

A STRANGER.

He doth not speak our language, but his ways
　　And manners have a charm that is their own,
Though etiquette is yet to him unknown ;
　　But all the household welcome him with praise,
For him bear lengthened watch and weary days,
　　If, in disquiet, he makes sound or moan ;
For him are gentle words and speech alone
　　Whose trust none save the recreant betrays !
He largess claims by right of birth divine.
　　A royal guest, he comprehendeth well,
Though all unskilled and innocent of art,
　　Love's atmosphere, and largess gives with sign,
In smiles and dimples his content to tell.
　　Though but a babe untaught, he reads the heart.

A WOMAN OF 1894.

She studies all the questions of the day,
And gives these problems of her earnest thought;
Wise plans for woman unto her are brought,
Which shed new light on her advancing way,
Or promise, for her weal, support and stay.
So, helped and helping, she herself is taught,
And serving others, honor wears, unsought,
When women meet in glad and proud array.
Though cultured, she has lost no winning grace,
Still, in the home, she leaves untried no art —
The home, where wife and mother, Heaven-sent,
Finds still her crown of life and highest place,
And the head bows before the shrine of heart.
Honor and hail ! We greet our President.

MRS. CLEVELAND'S PICTURE.

Beside the Nation's Chief is thy high place,
But not for this I love to look on thee,
'Tis for the noble vision that I see,
Of winsome womanhood and peerless grace.
With changing charm unfolding is the trace,
In mien mature, of Nature's royalty,
The dawning of yet nobler life to be,
With motherhood divine in thy young face.
No laureate is ours thy praise to sing,
No pomp of court or palace to be thine,
But stately in thy robing's fitting sheen,
To thee Columbia's women fair shall bring,
From countless hearths, their tributes to thy shrine
Of love and home and land to crown thee queen !

THE MADISON SQUARE TOWER.

After long months, again within the square
I stood, when lo ! before me, on the sky,
Where naught had been, in iris tracery,
Loomed, as by magic art, a structure fair,
A Campanile, vision of the air,
With bluest heaven its tints in harmony ;
And, gleaming golden, on its crescent high,
Diana's form of grace beyond compare.
Its fairy loggias the clouds do span,
A wondrous tale of perfect art to tell,
At eve, at noon, and rosy dawn of day.
Is it indeed the work of hand of man,
Or are we under wizard's mystic spell,
And it but mirage soon to steal away ?

———————

YESTERDAY, TO-DAY AND TO-MORROW.

The book of life lay closed at dead of night :
When o'er the earth, afresh, with golden ray,
Aurora flooded all the heavenly way.
I sought the volume for the page so white
On its blank surface fairest thought to write,
When, lo ! already, clouds and mists of gray
Were on the leaf inscribed from yesterday,
But mingled with a halo fair of light.
So know I well, that when another morn
In tints of pearl and beauty shall arise,
To-day's dark hues or colors fair shall lend
To the fresh page that I shall seek at dawn
Commingled ill and good before my eyes,
And retrospect of pain and joy shall blend !

WHAT I HAVE HAD.

No matter what the future hath in store,
Nought can deprive me of the happy past,
While life itself and memory shall last.
The vanished hours, with friends gone on before,
In golden days that are for me no more,
Secure in fond remembrances are cast.
Nor are they lost, who, in an unknown vast,
Have wandered far, our dearest, from time's shore.
For if, in garden of Gethsemane,
I drank, in agony, a cup of woe,
And walked in shade and darkness of the night,
It has been mine a vision rare to see,
It has been mine a love divine to know,
And I have stood, entranced, on Pisgah's height.

POETRY.

Ethereal alchemist, whose touch so fine
To lovely shapes transmuteth common things,
And over all a rainbow halo flings
Of tints supernal that resplendent shine,
From Helicon thou comest: from the Nine
Two forms attend, and low to thee one sings,
And one doth compass thee with outspread wings,
When thou dost soar to realm of light divine.
Through the blue ether swift the trio float,
With rich gifts laden, to the haunts of men,
But seeking beauty's source as steadfast goal,
While Music ceaseless trills her sweetest note,
And Art her pinions white unfolds again,
Bearing aloft, of all things fair, the Soul!

HYMETTUS.

" A dream of man and woman,
Diviner, but still human."

HYMETTUS.

ACT FIRST.—*Scene First*.

(A small dwelling, in an olive grove, near Athens.
ISMENE, a young girl, with her father's sister,
DAPHNE.

Daphne.—How the time speeds; it seems but yester-
day
Thy father, Lycon, placed thee in my care,
To train thee as thy mother would have done,
Thy fair, sweet mother, whom the gods did love,—
So early snatched from earth. Thy father wise,
A statesman learned, whom all at Athens knew,
He did entreat me with his dying breath,
To bring thee up as should become his child.
But yesterday the news sped forth abroad,
That thou the poor young sculptor soon wouldst wed.
Thou, the great Lycon's only child, wilt stoop
To marry one to wealth and fame unknown,
Thou shouldst have questioned of the oracle,
But list! who comes? I hear a step outside.

> Enter POLYGNOTUS, famous painter, whom
> DAPHNE receives with reverence. ISMENE bows
> low.

Polygnotus.—The spirit of dead Lycon calls me here,
To speak a word of warning to his child.

A rumor hath gone forth in Athens' streets,
That soon Hymettus, alien and unknown,
Doth wed Ismene, Lycon's only child.
'Tis not a nuptial that the gods approve.
Ismene.—And why?
Polyg.—Why? Why? Hymettus is so young,
His name and fortune all unknown to fame,
A child astray, found at the mountain's base,
Received its name, and nothing else is known,
Save that his parents in their distant home
Died, leaving but the yearling to the care
Of one who since hath died. His lineage
No one can tell, nor long he here hath dwelt.
'Tis but twice twenty months since first he came
To bide with us, alone, a stripling then,
To serve as model for great Phidias.
His perfect limbs, his noble shape did make
Proportion for Apollo's god-like form;
His very features, e'en the head's fine poise,
Are reproduction of Hymettus' own.
Ism.—What then? Is this not honor? Wouldst
      thou say
That old Basillus, with his shriveled limbs,
Were worthier to wed?
Polyg.—Hinder me not.
I do but own the beauty of the youth
Whom thou hast chosen: noble model he,—
A student, too, of art; with the soft clay
He doth attempt his master's skill to learn.
A visionary youth, he hath done naught

To merit yet Ismene's honored hand,
Nor parents hath to find him friends and means.
Thou shouldst consult the oracle, I say,
And then think well.

Daphne.—'Tis thus I did advise.

> Enter CHRYSILLA, DIANA and CLEMANTHE, IS-
> MENE'S friends, who greet her warmly.

Clemanthe.—We come to offer joyful wish to thee,
Since thou so happy art. We join in praise,
When youth and love and beauty such as thine
Shall wed with youth and beauty like to that
The gods on young Hymettus have bestowed.

Diana.—So gifted, too !

Clem.—His name shall be as famed
As his great master's, in the gods' good time !

Ism.—Thanks, O kind friends !

> Enter LABDA, old and of stern visage.

Labda.—I hope I'm not too late
To speak a word into Ismene's ear.
Wed not the young Hymettus ! dost thou know
That strange, insidious disease may lurk
To leave thee widowed, in thy fair young prime?
His parents died when he was but a babe,
An alien he to Anthens and her ways.

> Enter PHIDIAS.

Ism. (aside)—What now? blow hot, blow cold—
which shall it be ?

Phidias to *Ismene.*—
A word with thee. A word have I of praise
For thy wise choice. Hymettus I commend—

91

My pupil now.   At length he may outstrip
The master he doth serve.   Thou doest well
To mate thy life with one so rich in gifts.

ISMENE draws herself up, and turns to her aunt.

Ism.—Consult the oracle, thou tellest me !
(*To Polyg.*)—Consult the oracle, thou sayest, too,
And then think well.—I follow this advice ;
An oracle I do consult,—my heart.
What doth it tell me ?   That my love is young,
Is fault that time will mend.   That he is poor
In worldly goods is true indeed,—too true,
But rich he is in all that makes a man !
Unknown to fame as yet, but dowered well,
Acknowledged now by Phidias himself.
His parents dead, and poor indeed in friends,—
So much the more he needeth all I give.
And if his health prove frail, a woman true
Should not desert him on so frail a charge.
Who knoweth length of life ? for none can tell
Whether our days be many or be few ;
If they be lived aright, it is enough.
Daphne.—The *oracle* can tell.
Ism.—I ask it not.
My heart shall be my oracle and guide.
It bids me keep my troth.   Perchance, in faith,
The oracles themselves had differed, too,
As you, my friends, have differed in your speech.
For so much kind intent I thank you all !
Daphne.—We waste our speech ;
The wedding robe prepared,—the rosy wine

92

Waits the libation ceremonial.
But not as other maidens doth she wed,
Who chooseth for herself an alien mate.
Better the Corinth trader; he at least
Hath slaves and wealth, and all things meet for her.

Scene Second.

A poor house in one of the poorest streets of
Athens. HYMETTUS and ISMENE.

Hym.—How likest thou the place? doth it seem poor?
In truth it was the smallest I could find.
Dost miss the olive groves?
Ism.—How fair they were!
But this is home,—our home,—I like it well.
Hym.—lt is not worthy thee.   But yesternight,
After my long day's toil with Phidias,
I left the market place, and strolled along
The stately streets, so dusty all the day:
I bared my head to catch the evening breeze,
And, petassus in hand, I wandered where
Munychia's slope, with marble temple crowned,
Showed rows of noble dwellings; there methought
Were mansions worthy of Ismene fair,
And as I gazed on one, with figures brown
'Gainst the white marble's dazzling background's gleam,
Behold, Basillus at its entrance stood,
And urged on me to enter,—round the court,
'Mid play of cooling fountains, opened rooms,
Each richer than the last, on colonnade.
Within the pillared peristyle, the birds

Did flit about with warble sweet and song,
And rich the hangings falling to the floor,
While fringed and scarlet divans offered rest.
And here, the table laid, a feast prepared,
Were slaves awaiting but a beck to serve.
Basillus urged refreshments,—bade me stay,—
I pleaded that Ismene looked for me.
But when I spoke thy name, he bid me bide
But yet a little, till he told to me
That ere a moon had waned, a bride should come
To brighten with her presence all his life.
Whom dost thou think will wed the rich old man ?
Ism.—Whom ?
Hym.—One of thy friends, Chrysilla, young and fair.
Ism.—Thou dost but jest, Hymettus ; surely she
Will never wed Basillus. Think it not.
Hym.—'Tis true. His gold hath charmed her parents'
    eyes.
She doth but do their bidding. Blame her not,
She is so young, in truth, and fair as young.
Ism.—To wed the Corinth trader, him who in
The foul macellum passed his length of days !
Hym.—For but a little time he bartered flesh
And fish,—then rose above his fellows near,
And dealt in costly fabrics. Merchant ships
Were his, which plied the deep and brought his wares
To Athens, and his coffers filled with gold ;
And long his trains of mules from town to town
With carpets from Miletus, grapes from Rhodes,
And sheen of silk from Corinth. Egypt, too,

Had stores for him,— papyrus,—and his wealth
Doubled and trebled with his forethought keen.
Would I could give to thee a home like his!
Ism.—Better a home like this, so bare, so plain,
With thee and love, than dwelling grander far
Than that Basillus giveth to his mate.
Hym.—If but my hand had made the cella's frieze!
'Tis work to be immortal.
Ism.—Dost thou not
Assist in all the toil of Phidias?
Hym.—Ay, but a name I covet for myself.
Ism.—But thou hast wondrous skill.   'Twas yesterday
Within thy ergasterion I stood,
And saw thy model and its perfect shape,
Majestic in its fine proportions all,
Its face so still, so sweet—I held my breath,
Nor spake nor moved—its quiet in my soul,
When at the threshold, grave, stood Phidias
With face intent.   'Tis Muta, then he said;
The goddess *Silence!* Wonderful the work
Hymettus has brought forth.   Rare pupil he
Who models such a face and form as this.
'Twill bring Hymettus fame, at length I said,
And fortune?
        Doubt it not; for, once his name
Is known as Muta's sculptor through the land,
He shall have gold and Athens at his feet.
Hym.—Praise from great Phidias is praise indeed.
Honor for thee, Ismene, do I crave,
Honor and wealth and slaves at thy command.

Ism.—Ah me ! I fear me lest the future bring
Some stealing shade, some loss, some phantom ill.
Hym.—Thy fears are womanish and weak—no more
Give counsel to them ; rather urge me on
To place my name on fame's immortal scroll.

ACT SECOND.—*Scene First.*

Elegant mansion in Munychia.

HYMETTUS, ISMENE and ALTHEA, a beautiful
child, six years old.

Hym.—At length I place thee in a fitting home,
The helots wait thy beck, and robes are thine
Rich as Chrysilla's, and they suit thy form.
Art thou not happy ?
Ism.—Wait. I cannot say,—
The quiet life, I loved it, loved it well.
But I am glad for thee. Sometimes indeed
The artist's fairest work lacks meed of praise.
Hym.—The quiet life of home shall still be ours,
Who have no relatives, nor friends nor foes
To do us honor or to work us woe.
Ism.—Thou now hast Fame. Through Athens' dusty
streets
And in the market place Hymettus' praise
Is borne from ear to ear.

Enter slave who hands billet to HYMETTUS.

A note for thee.
Hym. (reads)—Great Phidias requesteth me to sup.

Enter slave with notes, and *notes* and *notes*.

Hym. (looks over and reads)—Basillus, Micon and a
    dozen more

The honor of my company entreat.

Nestor, who knew me not in former day,

Now begs that I will deign to visit him,

If I will condescend to his abode.

Ism. (aside)—And this is fame !

Enter slave with more notes.

Hym.(reads)—

" The ties of blood are ever honored ones ;

We find that we thy loving kinsfolk are.

We crave the great Hymettus famed to know,

To whom the gods so generous have been.

But meagerly they have endowered us ;

Yet are we not to Nelid blood allied ? "

(signed) Alcmæon.

Hym. (reads again)—

" Your spreading fame hath sounded in our ears ;

We crave your help, who are so greatly blessed,

Since of your house and lineage we come.

A widow I, once wife of Danaos,

With children six to rear up for the state.

We are your relatives, and claim your care."

(signed) Isodice.

HYMETTUS throws down a dozen more.

Hym.—They all crave help from me and claim me
    now,

A tie of blood I never knew before ;

An orphan boy, alone I fought my way.

Ism.—And this is Fame !

97

Enter ICTINUS, an architect.

Ictinus.—To Athens just returned, I paused beside
A group of strangers, over whom a hush
Profound had settled. What, methought, is here
That causeth reverence and stillness deep?
Behold, 'twas Muta's statue. I, too, stood,
Transfixed before the beauty of her face.
O, wonderful the art that maketh men
Pause from their busy ways awhile to learn
Of beauty, art, and majesty of peace.
I asked the artist's name, and one stepped forth,—
'Twas Polygnotus ;—'twas his pride, he said,
To tell me of Hymettus, alien once,
But gladly now doth Athens call him son.
Ism.—But this *is* Fame !

(ALTHEA runs to Ictinus and says :)

Hymettus is my father, and I'm glad.

Slave brings billet to ISMENE, who reads :

"Daphne is glad that Lycon's only child
Is joined to one so great. She doeth well
Who weds Hymettus, and I greeting send
With kindly messages to her and him."
Hym.—Daphne !
Ism.—Daphne !
The times are changed indeed !

Scene Second.—Olympus.

Gods and Goddesses.

Jupiter.—What news of Hellas? Athens " violet
crowned " ?
What has befallen swift-winged Mercury ?

98

Jup.—What tidings bringest thou? Why this delay?
Mercury.—Have I not sped with ever flying feet
Over the purple hills, o'er sheen of sea,
O'er far Arcadian mounts, where whitest snow
Lies ever on the peak of Taygetus?
Through richest demes, past Pentelicus,
Where gleams the pure white marble in its breast,
Roaming o'er Helicon, with verdure clad,
Climbing Parnassus steep, and on again
To Mount Hymettus, where the bees do make
Honey as sweet as nectar? From the side
Of Mount Pentelicus, through richest plain
Of Kephissus to groves of Academe,
To the bare hills round Athens' busy streets?
It was a festal day,—the peplus borne
(Broidered by maids on the Acropolis),
To Athene, within the Parthenon,
Of gold and ivory, wrought by Phidias.
Jup.—Hast word of mortal?
Mer.—Yes, Hymettus young
Hath carved the form of Muta,—'tis a form
Worthy the workmanship of Phidias.
Jup.—Hast aught of life or death? the pallid Mors
Hath brought a being fair to dwell with us.
Mer.—'Tis Althea. But now I saw the home
Made desolate. Ismene's bloom has fled.
Hymettus' hand hath lost its skill and art.
Juno.—His hand hath lost its art? Great Jove,
    endow

This sculptor noble with another gift.
Make him a poet. Give him beauty's love :
Let him enkindle it in other hearts.
He suffers : from his deeps of agony,
Let him heal hearts as heavy as his own.
Minerva.—Think yet again, great Juno, once again,
Ere thou shalt give him food from Helicon.
His eye will seek for beauty everywhere,
His ear will long for harmony divine.
His soul, attuned to heavenly cadences,
How will it bear the jar and fret of earth ?
How shall he be misunderstood by men !
Juno.—Thy words bear weight of wisdom, yet were
    earth
All too prosaic were not glimpses given
From other worlds, to lighten all its cares.
Min.—Great Jove revealed himself to Phidias,
And he shall die in prison. Socrates
Shall drink the hemlock, and our Pericles
Weeps before dicasts, pleading for his love.
Jup.—Juno, a poet soul doth Athens need.
Endow Hymettus. Send unto his home
The drowsy Somnus, and let muses twain
Attend his flight with draught from Helicon.
Let Calliope and Erato be called.
The Fury Tisiphone (aside).—A good day's doing !
    He shall suffer now !
Ha ! those fine nerves shall throb in direst pain !
Jup.—What of Ismene ?
Juno.—Have no fear for her ;

'Tis true, the weary watch has snatched her bloom,
And earth is desolate ; but here with us
Her fair young daughter dwells, and tenderly,
With cords of love, she draws her mother's heart,

Scene Third—Hymettus' Home.

(ISMENE pale and haggard. HYMETTUS sleeping.
He wakens and presses hand to his head)

Hym.—Such a deep sleep! There came an incense
strange,
Like breath of thousand scarlet poppies, borne
Around me, and a wingèd god appeared
And carried me up to Parnassus' heights,
Where two fair nymphs, in robes diaphanous,
Attended me with draught from Helicon.
I waken here, but in my fecund brain
Are seething fancies, music, rhythm, and thoughts
Too great for speech, and longing to create.
Ism.—Write down the record, for mayhap the gods
Have given thee a message unto men.

(HYMETTUS retires to write. Slave enters with
note.

Ism. (reads)—" Great Pericles from Delphic oracle
A message hath received. The word is this :
Hymettus hath been given from on high
A gift of poesy, and at the grand
Panathenaic festival 'tis meet
That all may hear Hymettus' word inspired."

101

(HYMETTUS enters and ISMENE shows the missive.)

Hym.—'Tis true.   The thoughts came from my burning brain
With words and rhythm and eloquence inspired.
Ism.—Thy brow is heated.   Leave thy work and go
Out in the cool night air, and come refreshed
To slumber ere thou writest more.   Away !

(HYMETTUS walks forth until he comes to Basillus' home. He enters. Chrysilla, radiantly beautiful, in exquisite chiton and peplus, dazzles him. She treats him with greatest deference. He feasts his eyes on her beauty.)

Chrys.—Our home ne'er had this honor great before!
Athens' own poet !   At the festival
('Tis well announced) we all shall hear thy song.
Wilt thou not write some lines for me, I pray?
Hym.—Nay, rather let me sit but at thy feet,
That in thy eyes I gain a vision new
Of beauty, that my inmost, kindling soul
Is fed on,—'tis like draught from Helicon.
Chrys.—Basillus loves not beauty,—more he loves
His obols and his demes.   Would the gods
But visit him with gifts.   Alas !   Alas !
I fear me they will never dwell with him !

(Enter BASILLUS, who greets HYMETTUS.)

Bas.—1 sought you in the market place with thought
To give you opportunity to buy
The lands you looked at, and I offer you
The purchase with but little gain for me.

(He draws out papers, and HYMETTUS makes purchase).

Hym.—The time doth press. Chrysilla, then good-
night.
Good-night, Basillus, and to-morrow morn
The land is mine, the money shall be thine.

Scene Fourth.

The Market Place.

Citizen.—Hast heard the news?
Second Citizen.—What news dost mean, I pray?
Cit.—Dost know Hymettus, the great poet, who
The drama for the Odeum composed,
When the vast multitude did list entranced?
Basillus him accuses, and before
The dicasts he shall answer for his crime.
Second Cit.—What crime hath he committed?
First Cit.—Knowest thou
That day by day he seeks Chrysilla's home;
That he, by art, hath sought and gained her love;
That she is faithless to her wedded mate?
Ict.—'Tis false! 'tis false! I know Hymettus well!
And well Basillus old I know—too well.
He'd sell his soul to make one obol more.
The worthless lands Hymettus bought of him
Have beggared him,—a poet, knowing naught
Of market values; and Ismene dwells
Within the modest home she knew as bride,
Her mansion gone, her helots now for sale.

103

I'll stake my faith Basillus doth to-day
Calumniate Hymettus and his wife.
Go through the streets and tell to whom you meet
What one of Athens' architects doth say;
He brands as infamous the tale that's told.
Hymettus, poet, loving all things fair,
Is innocent and guileless as a child.
Haye you not heard him on the bema, friends?
Didst hear his drama at the Odeum,
When thousands thronged to catch his living words?
Cit.—Ay, 'twas a matchless play, but quick to blame
As quick to praise are the Athenians,
And old Basillus venom hath and wealth.
The dicasts may be bought by Corinth gold.
Ict.—It shall not be! Again it shall not be!
The gods who him endowed shall prove his faith!

Scene Fifth.

ISMENE's home. Small dwelling where she lived
when first married.
HYMETTUS bowed in grief.

Hym.—And I have brought you to this dismal home!
A curse upon the gods who gifted me
With all unfitness for this earth!—For see,
My own true wife must suffer by my side.
Ism.—Nay, 'tis not so! A noble gift is thine.
Thy words are solace to the sorrowing,
And fraught with joy to the Athenians.
I love this home the more, for here began
Our nuptials, and Althea entered life.

Hym.—When all the dicasts shall have judged me ill,—

Ism.—They cannot judge thee ill! Thou hast done naught.

Hym.—Thou knowest the Athenians, so quick
To crown with honor, or to blast with shame.

Ism.—Then wherefore heed them? Thou hast many friends,
And come what may, we cannot parted be.
Tell me the tale Hymettus. Well I know
How thou art wronged of money thou hadst earned.
But that is small account. Be thou content,
And I shall miss nor mansion fair nor slave;
But tell me of Chrysilla,—how it is
That old Basillus dares asperse thy name.

Hym.—Thou knowest, when the gods had dowered me
With thirst for beauty, all things fair I loved,
Embodiment Chrysilla seemed to me
Of all that I had sought, so day by day
I looked upon her beauteous eyes to see
The soul within that dwelt harmonious
With such a fair outside—a sacred shrine
Where gods might more reveal themselves to men.
So eve and noon I sought her presence bright,
When, speeding there one morn, I met my friend,
Ictinus, whom thou knowest good and true.
" And whither goest thou? " he said to me.
" To talk with fair Chrysilla," I replied.
" Thou wastest speech," he answered; " hast thou not
A higher task that's given thee to do?
Dost mind the praise of little Althea,

'Hymettus is my father, and I'm glad '?''
At those sweet words, by chance brought back to me—
Ism.—Oh, say not chance !
Hym.—I pondered, pondered well,
Whether the carmine cheeks, the sparkling eyes
Were mated with a soul as rare as thine,
So steadfast, true, behind thy pale, smooth brow.
So pondering, I gave him my reply—
" Chrysilla is my friend—a friend like thee."
" 'Tis true, and I who know thee, love thee well ;
But thou art not like others, and their tongues
Will tell ill tales of thee ; Basillus, too,
Will vent his anger and his spleen on thee."
This is the tale.   I visited no more
Chrysilla's home.   Full well I know, my wife,
That rarer powers enfolded are in thee.

(They embrace.)
(Enter messenger with billet.)

Ism.—The dicasts' judgment ! oh, my trembling hands
Scarce dare to venture ?   Courage !   I *will* read !

ISMEN reads.

The heliasts Hymettus do adjudge
To go to Gaius, in Arcadia,
Before the priestess, and take draught of blood,
Upon his oath of innocence.   'Tis known
That whoso perjureth shall die at once.
If he survive this test, then shall to him
His money from Basillus be restored.
Ism.—Oh, dicasts wise !
The gods above make known his innocence !

106

Last Scene.

(Gaius, in Arcadia.)

(Temple with priestess, rites prepared. Athenian citizens, Hermippus, Ictinus, Phidias, and others. Hymettus and Ismene side by side. Daphne enters. Basillus watches Hymettus and Ismene malignantly.)

Cit.—All things on earth may righted be at last,
If we but bide our time. Hymettus here
So long has praised and flattered been, we tire
Of all the titles added to his name.

(HERMIPPUS, who has been reproved for his comedies.)

If he had been less grave, of lighter mind,
'Twere better for him. Down with him, I say !
Cit.—Look at Basillus, with his evil eyes !
Second Cit.—Behold Ismene's face ! her brow as calm
As 'twere a festal day. An hour hence
A front of shame and sorrow she may wear.
Phidias.—No shame to her or hers, whate'er betide !
Before the gods each soul alone doth show !
Third Cit.—At early morn, on the Acropolis,
I saw the owls by scores, and watched their flight,
And knew the omen evil, and I heard
The tellix, with its shrill, discordant cry.
The cap of clouds, on Erymanthus' peak,
Is thick and dark, and soon will come the storm.
Hymettus hath but harbingers of ill.
Daphne.—We all did warn Ismene and did fear
The alien youth. *I doubt not he will die !*
Ict.—Behold who comes. 'Tis Pericles himself !

Ism. (to Hym.)—The priestess comes ! the draught
  will be prepared !
'Tis but a moment, and the gracious gods
Will unto all declare thy innocence :
Ism. (to Ictinus)—Is it not so, dear friend ?
Ict.—I cannot say.
Ism.—What dost thou mean, my friend ? what canst
  thou mean ?
Ict.—No doubt about Hymettus,—innocent
And guileless ever as a little child.
But do we know decision of the gods ?
Through Eleusinian way, in niches placed,
To Nemesis are votive tablets set
By order of Basillus, and his tongue
Doth change Hymettus' friends to bitter foes.

(Ismene grows pallid and totters.)

Ism.—Just Gods ! Great Jove ! What hope is left to
  us,
If Nemesis against us is allied ?
First Cit.—Look at Ismene now ! She totters, faints !
Second Cit.—But for a moment, and she braves again.
And see, about her cluster Phidias,
And Socrates, and Polygnotus famed,
And look again, great Pericles himself,
With message from the Delphic oracle !
Basillus (to Hym.)—If thou hast aught to say, take
  now the time,
If thou hast thought of wife or property.
The gods shall strike with instant death who dares
To take false oath with draught of bullock's blood.

Hym.—Naught say I unto you.   My innocence
Is known and shall be proven by the gods.

      (PERICLES comes forth.)

Per.—On white Parnassus lies the drifting snow,
Whence cometh message from the Delphic fane
Before the cup he quaffs.   Oh, listen well.
Thus reads the oracle : No man shall fall
Who loves with constancy a little child.
The gods themselves shall dwell with him who has
A child he loves in the Empyrean !
Ism.—Our Althea hath saved thee.   Joy, oh, joy !
Drink quickly ! quaff the cup ! proclaim thy faith !

      (HYMETTUS takes the goblet and holds it.)

Bas.—He hesitates.   He knoweth well the power
Held by great Nemesis o'er Jove himself !
Hym.—Nothing I fear, albeit life or death
Lieth in waiting in these rosy dregs.
One word, Ismene :   To the poet soul,
Hadst thou a doubt,—a faintest doubt,—made known,
A deadly essence, poisoning all love
And faith between us,—then were all things fair,
E'en the bright sunshine, turned to darkest night.
But thou, O true and noble one, hast shown
The perfect love that knows nor doubt nor shade,
An intellect too large to gauge and mete,
With petty bonds, a nature different,
And whether Nemesis be great, or Jove,
I know Heaven now, in thy undying love.

      (He quaffs and lives.   The people now applaud.)

Per.—Hymettus lives ! his innocence is proved !
Athens rejoices for her honored son !
Basillus now the dicasts must obey ;
The worthless lands must be redeemed again.
Daphne.—The lands shall be redeemed ! Ah, well, I'm
glad
I *ever did befriend* the *alien youth!*
Ism.—Yet let him keep his wealth ! we need it not,
Who treasures own that he may never know !

www.ingramcontent.com/pod-product-compliance
Lightning Source LLC
Chambersburg PA
CBHW022145020726
47496CB00008B/2563